Amy's Big Race

The Sound of Long A

by Cecilia Minden and Joanne Meier • illustrated by Bob Ostrom

The Child's World

Published by The Child's World®
1980 Lookout Drive
Mankato, MN 56003-1705
800-599-READ
www.childsworld.com

The Child's World®: Mary Berendes, Publishing Director
The Design Lab: Design and page production

Library of Congress Cataloging-in-Publication Data
Minden, Cecilia.
  Amy's big race : the sound of long a / by Cecilia
Minden and Joanne Meier ; illustrated by Bob Ostrom.
     p. cm.
  ISBN 978-1-60253-393-6 (library bound : alk. paper)
  1. English language—Vowels—Juvenile literature. 2.
English language—Phonetics—Juvenile literature 3.
Reading—Phonetic method—Juvenile literature. I. Meier,
Joanne D. II. Ostrom, Bob. III. Title.
  PE1157.M563 2010
  428.1—dc22   2010002907

Printed in the United States of America in Mankato, MN.
July 2010
F11538

NOTE TO PARENTS AND EDUCATORS:

The Child's World® has created this series with the goal of exposing children to engaging stories and illustrations that assist in phonics development. The books in the series will help children learn the relationships between the letters of written language and the individual sounds of spoken language. This contact helps children learn to use these relationships to read and write words.

The books in this series follow a similar format. An introductory page, to be read by an adult, introduces the child to the phonics feature, or sound, that will be highlighted in the book. Read this page to the child, stressing the phonic feature. Help the student learn how to form the sound with her mouth. The story and engaging illustrations follow the introduction. At the end of the story, word lists categorize the feature words into their phonic elements.

Each book in this series has been carefully written to meet specific readability requirements. Close attention has been paid to elements such as word count, sentence length, and vocabulary. Readability formulas measure the ease with which the text can be read and understood. Each book in this series has been analyzed using the Spache readability formula.

Reading research suggests that systematic phonics instruction can greatly improve students' word recognition, spelling, and comprehension skills. This series assists in the teaching of phonics by providing students with important opportunities to apply their knowledge of phonics as they read words, sentences, and text.

The letter a makes two sounds.

The short sound of **a** sounds like **a** as in: *cat* and *add*.

The long sound of **a** sounds like **a** as in: *cake* and *date*.

In this book, you will read words that have the long **a** sound as in: *race, lake, waves,* and *place.*

Today is the big race.

Amy is in the race.

She wakes up early.

She can't be late!

The race is around the lake.

Amy hopes she wins the race!

Amy goes to the gate.

Her name is on the list.

Amy waves to her friends.

They came to race, too.

Amy takes her place in line.

They all begin to race.

The kids run fast around the lake. Amy takes the lead. She runs very fast.

Will she win?

Will she take first place?

Amy wins the race!

She has a big smile

on her face!

Fun Facts

Did you know that Lake Baikal is the deepest lake in the world and is located in Russia? Lake Superior is the largest freshwater lake in the world and touches the states of Michigan, Wisconsin, Minnesota, and part of Canada. The Dead Sea in Israel is called a sea but is actually a lake. It is the lowest lake in the world. It is also the saltiest—hardly any plants or animals are able to live in it!

You have to be a great runner to compete in some races! Long-distance races are called *marathons*. They date back to the modern Olympic Games held in Athens, Greece, in the late 1800s. The oldest and most famous marathon is the Boston Marathon. It is run in Boston, Massachusetts. Runners travel more than 26 miles (42 kilometers) in this race.

Activity

A Picnic by the Lake

If the weather is warm and sunny, pack a picnic basket with your family and head toward the shore of a nearby lake. Don't forget to bring a blanket, sunscreen, and your favorite foods. Some activities you could try include swimming, fishing, or going for a boat ride.

To Learn More

Books
About the Sound of Long A
Moncure, Jane Belk. *My "a" Sound Box®*. Mankato, MN: The Child's World, 2009.

About Lakes
Barnes, Julia. *101 Facts about Lakes*. Milwaukee, WI: Gareth Stevens, 2004.

Holland, Simon, and Anna Lofthouse. *Eye Wonder: Rivers and Lakes*. New York: DK Publishing, 2003.

Wood, John Norris, and Kevin Dean. *Rivers & Lakes*. Denton, TX: Mathew Price, 2009.

About Races
Carlson, Nancy L. *Loudmouth George and the Big Race*. Minneapolis, MN: Carolrhoda Books, 2004.

Ostrow, Kim, Clint Bond (illustrator), and Andy Clark (illustrator). *The Great Snail Race*. New York: Scholastic, 2005.

Wolff, Ashley. *Stella & Roy*. New York: Penguin, 1996.

Web Sites
Visit our home page for lots of links about the Sound of Long A:
childsworld.com/links

Note to Parents, Teachers, and Librarians: We routinely check our Web links to make sure they're safe, active sites—so encourage your readers to check them out!

Long A
Feature Words

Proper Names
Amy

**Feature Words with the
Consonant-Vowel-Silent E
Pattern**

came
face
gate
lake
late
race
take
wake
wave

**Feature Words with Other
Long Vowel Pattern**
today

About the Authors

Cecilia Minden, PhD, is the former director of the Language and Literacy Program at the Harvard Graduate School of Education. She is now a reading consultant for school and library publications. She earned her PhD in reading education from the University of Virginia. Cecilia and her husband, Dave Cupp, live outside Chapel Hill, North Carolina. They enjoy sharing their love of reading with their grandchildren, Chelsea and Qadir.

Joanne Meier, PhD, has worked as an elementary school teacher, university professor, and researcher. She earned her BA in early childhood education from the University of South Carolina, and her MEd and PhD in education from the University of Virginia. She currently works as a literacy consultant for schools and private organizations. Joanne lives in Virginia with her husband Eric, daughters Kella and Erin, two cats, and a gerbil.

About the Illustrator

Bob Ostrom has been illustrating children's books for nearly twenty years. A graduate of the New England School of Art & Design at Suffolk University, Bob has worked for such companies as Disney, Nickelodeon, and Cartoon Network. He lives in North Carolina with his wife Melissa and three children, Will, Charlie, and Mae.